The WAY of the
SHEPHERD

The WAY of the

A Story of

SHEPHERD

the Twenty-third Psalm

written and illustrated
by NORA S. UNWIN

McGRAW-HILL BOOK COMPANY, Inc.
NEW YORK   TORONTO   LONDON

Acknowledgment

The author is most grateful to her good friend Elizabeth Yates, for her ever-ready help and encouragement; and to the Zion Research Library of Brookline, Massachusetts, for their valuable assistance in providing books and other materials relative to life in the Holy Land.

To

W. & E.

with love and gratitude

The Lord is my shepherd.

Wrapped in his thick coat, young Azor stirred and felt the ground, hard beneath him. He opened his eyes. Where was he? The darkness was huge above him. What millions of stars there were! A lamb bleated. Was it lonesome too? Now he remembered. Reuben the shepherd, his father's old friend, was close by, sleeping at the door of the fold. When dawn broke they would start work together, and he would learn from Reuben the skills of a shepherd.

Would it be hard? Would he be scared out on the hills?

The quiet old shepherd looked kind, but Azor could not help thinking of his mother and father back home in the village. In all his nine years he had never been far from them. He slept fitfully and dreamed of his mother spinning wool.

Sometime later a shepherd's horn echoed across the valley. Then Azor heard Reuben calling, *"Taa-taa, Ho! Ho! Ho!"* The day was beginning.

Azor hurried to the well where he found the old shepherd, who greeted him kindly.

The water felt cold but, following Reuben's example, Azor splashed some over his face, then drank a cupful.

"You shall carry our provisions for the day," said Reuben, putting a leather bag over the boy's shoulder. "Now let us say our prayer together, son, the song of David, the shepherd boy."

"The one we said last night?"

"Aye, and the one we'll say tonight and every morning too."

They stood together while the sheep in the fold close by remained quiet, as if they were listening. Slowly Reuben recited while Azor joined in where he could remember—

"The Lord is my shepherd; I shall not want.

"He maketh me to lie down in green pastures: he leadeth me beside the still waters. He restoreth my soul: he leadeth me in the paths of righteousness for his name's sake.

"Yea, though I walk through the valley of the shadow of death, I will fear no evil: for thou art with me; thy rod and thy staff they comfort me.

"Thou preparest a table before me in the presence of mine enemies: thou anointest my head with oil; my cup runneth over.

"Surely goodness and mercy shall follow me all the days of my life: and I will dwell in the house of the Lord for ever."

Standing beside Reuben, Azor sensed how strong and quiet the old man was. He suddenly felt safe and happy with him.

I shall not want.

"Now it is time to lead the flock out," said Reuben.

Standing at the entrance of the walled fold, he called till the sheep clustered toward him. Then, picking up his long staff, he turned and led the way. His thick rod hung from his belt. Azor walked at his side while the sheep followed, one by one, through the narrow stone doorway.

It was an orderly procession that trotted behind them in the gray light. The leader sheep wore a bell around its neck. Azor liked the bell's mellow note. Across the hills other sheep bells could be heard ringing. He wondered if there were boys with those flocks too.

"Where are we going?" he asked shyly.

"To yonder uplands." Reuben pointed ahead.

"Do the sheep know?"

"Maybe, maybe not, but they know they'll not want for food as long as they stay with me. Their day is all planned."

"Did you plan it?"

"Aye, that's a shepherd's work, Azor, to plan every night where he'll take his flock on the morrow. He plans so as to give them grazing and rest alternately through the day."

"I expect they are hungry already," said Azor. He knew that he was.

Soon they reached an open hillside. It was stony, but the grass was plentiful. Reuben sat down on a rock and laid his staff near him. The sheep dropped their heads and ate busily. Taking the leather bag, Reuben drew from it two round loaves. "Something for us too," he said.

Azor munched his loaf gratefully while he watched the lambs. They skipped so comically. He longed to play with them, but he sat as Reuben did and watched quietly. The sun had risen. Its warm rays flooded the hillside. Azor took off his coat. The coarse grass pricked his legs.

"How wiry the grass is! Do the sheep really like it?" he asked.

"Aye, it is coarse, but they like the early dew on it. Later they'll get some that's more tender."

Azor observed that Reuben's eyes never left the flock. Now and then the old shepherd spoke to the sheep tenderly and sometimes commandingly. They all faced in the same direction as they grazed, and Azor asked Reuben if they always did that.

"It's their custom," Reuben explained. "They follow their leader."

Azor saw that one sheep near the leader had a broken horn.

He maketh me to lie down in green pastures.

By now the sun was high overhead and the day was growing hot.

"It is time we moved on," said Reuben. He gave his call, *"Ho! Ho! Taa-taa,"* until every long face looked toward him. Then, staff in hand, he started down the hillside.

"We must go to a shady spot for the forenoon rest."

The sheep followed close behind. Azor noticed that the sheep with the broken horn was next to the leader. He recognized others, too, and questioned Reuben.

"Aye, that's their order for today. They'll keep those positions till day's end. You watch."

Soon they reached a valley where some large trees grew. The grass was green and lush.

"The sheep will like this," smiled Azor.

"They'll like it well enough," answered Reuben, "but it's

to rest in now, not to eat." Facing the flock, he lifted his staff and struck the leader lightly across the back. Then he rapped the five or six sheep nearest it.

"Why do you do that? asked Azor, in alarm.

"That's to tell them to lie down," said Reuben. "They must be made to rest now."

Obediently the first group of sheep folded their legs under them. Soon all did likewise.

Reuben leaned against a tree trunk; Azor joined him. The shade felt welcome. Now the sheep were peacefully chewing their cud while the lambs rested beside their mothers. Azor longed to hold a lamb. Reuben took out his shepherd's pipe and began to play. Azor liked the sound.

"The sheep enjoy it, too, don't they?"

"Aye, they do that," nodded the old man. "This is a good time of day. Now they are putting on fat; they are content."

He leadeth me beside the still waters.

Reuben spread out his thick coat on the ground and opened the bag which Azor had been carrying. The boy was glad it was their turn to eat. He saw that the pouch contained other things besides food supplies. Then he helped Reuben to lay their meal out on the coat. There were dates, goat cheese, six small loaves of bread, and a few green olives. After Reuben said a blessing, they ate unhurriedly.

"Thank you, Reuben," Azor said, wiping his mouth with the back of his hand. Never had food tasted better.

"The thanks aren't all mine, son." Then he spoke reverently: "He opens his hand and satisfies the need of every one of us."

After they had packed away the remains of their meal, Reuben said, "Now that the sheep are well rested, it is time that they drank. I don't doubt but that you are thirsty too?"

Azor donned the leather pouch as Reuben called to the flock. When all had responded, the shepherd led the way farther down the valley to where a stream flowed over a stony bed. The water gurgled as it fell into pools here and there. The sound frightened the sheep. They hesitated.

Reuben found a sheltered place where the water eddied slowly. He scooped up a cupful and studied it carefully; then he tasted it. Handing the cup to Azor, he said, "Drink some, it's good. But first pull me a handful of grass." Then, grass in hand, the shepherd enticed the leader and the first six sheep to follow him into the water. Now he stood and whistled: *"Tirr–r–r, tirr–r–r–r."*

That was a signal the sheep knew.

Immediately they drank eagerly. When the first six had quenched their thirst, Reuben called six more.

It took awhile till all the forty sheep had had their fill. Meanwhile, the old man told Azor to water the lambs from his cup.

Azor felt a thrill of pleasure as he held the cup to each velvet nose and coaxed the lambs to drink. He tried to imitate Reuben's low *"Tirr–r–r, tirr–r–r–r."*

He restoreth my soul.

For another hour or more they stayed in the valley. Reuben, sitting in the shade, watched, but Azor lay down. The hum of insects made him drowsy. Presently he heard a *Ba–a–aaa* close to his ear. He sat up. One sheep had left its place in the flock and was walking toward Reuben.

"What does it want?" asked Azor sleepily.

"You'll see," said Reuben softly. He held out his hand, beckoning the sheep nearer. It came close. Reuben ran his brown hand down the sheep's long nose, caressing its face and scratching its ears. He spoke to it affectionately in words that Azor could not understand. In response, the sheep rubbed its head against Reuben's shoulder, then playfully nibbled his ear.

Azor laughed. "Is this one a special pet?"

"Yes," replied Reuben. "But they are all my special pets. Look, here comes another." With a friendly pat on the rump, Reuben pushed the first sheep away to return to its place in the flock and called the other to come to him.

Next came a mother and her twin lambs for their share of attention. Reuben petted and talked to each one, whispering comfortable sheep language into their ears.

"May I pet one, too?" asked Azor hesitantly.

Reuben nodded.

One lamb skipped away shyly, but the other nuzzled Azor's hand.

"Do they always do this?" Azor asked happily, as he stroked the silky ears.

"Whenever they feel the need," said Reuben. "Perhaps they are weary or uneasy. Then a little talk—a bit of companionship—helps them through the long day." The ram was standing beside the shepherd now, nuzzling his hand. "Ours is a mightily close friendship, isn't it?" Reuben rubbed the ram's cheeks and Azor saw the answer in its trusting gaze.

Azor remembered there were times when he needed to be near his father—just watching him work or hearing his voice. At other times the warm feel of his mother's cheek or just knowing she was there in the house would cheer and comfort him.

"You are like both father and mother to them, aren't you, Reuben?"

"Aye, father and mother and friend," said the old man nodding.

*He leadeth me in the paths of righteousness
for His name's sake.*

"Do the sheep always follow you?" asked Azor. "Are they always good?"

"Nay, they have their own ways. Sometimes one can be as mischievous as a child," replied Reuben. "That's why I must keep watching them. Sometimes an imaginary thing can frighten them, often a real thing. Then the shepherd must work fast."

"With his staff?"

"Aye, and with his voice, and his rod, maybe. Once the sheep scatter, it's all the harder to unite them again. I learned that a long while ago, and I've never forgotten it."

As Reuben spoke he stood up. All the while he had been watching a lamb which was beginning to wander, heedless of its mother's urgent call.

"Bring me a stone, Azor," Reuben said, reaching for his sling. "Just a small one," he added, as he saw the anxiety on the boy's face.

Then with sure aim he whirled it into the air. It dropped harmlessly a few feet ahead of the lamb. That was enough. The thud of its landing startled the lamb and sent it running back to its mother's side.

Azor made up his mind to practice with his sling shot till he could aim as surely as Reuben.

Yea, though I walk through the valley
of the shadow of death,
I will fear no evil: for thou art with me.

The time for rest was over and Reuben prepared to leave the pleasant place. First he picked up several stones from the river bed and tucked them in the folds of his belt. "We have farther to go to reach our next pasture," he told Azor. "The grazing there is fine; but first we must pass through a narrow valley."

Azor looked ahead. The hills on each side seemed to join together before them. The sun was lost behind clouds now. It was much cooler. By the time they reached the narrow pass, a chill wind was blowing. Azor shivered. The dark hills seemed to tower over them. The rocks looked huge and forbidding.

"Do we *have* to go this way?" the boy asked.

"Aye, it's our way home from here."

Azor glanced back. The flock trotted along in a tight bunch, pressing close behind their shepherd. But as the pathway wound and twisted between great boulders, Azor lost sight of the last few sheep. Reuben began to whistle. He continually repeated his call: *"Taa-taa, Ho! Ho! Ho!"* Looking at Azor, he explained, "That tells those last ones I'm still here in front."

"I like to hear you whistle, too," said the boy. "It's comforting." He would like to have slipped his hand into Reuben's strong one, but the path was getting too rocky to walk abreast. His heart beat fast. He could imagine ugly things peering out of shadowy places. He noticed a strong queer smell. A vulture was wheeling in the sky above them.

"Are there wolves in this valley?" he asked.

"Yes, sometimes, and hyenas, but they appear only at night," said Reuben calmly. "There are other dangers to watch for now." Even as he spoke, a dark form, crouching low, slipped from behind a rock ahead of them. "Stand still, Azor, keep in front of the leader," he ordered.

Azor took a firm stand, though his knees felt weak.

Quickly Reuben's sling went into action. The howl of a wild dog echoed through the valley as it leaped high, then rolled over into a heap. Reuben ran forward and gave the creature a final blow with his club-ended rod. Azor shuddered, but he knew it had to be done.

The sheep were frightened, too, and began to jostle each other. Reuben mounted a high rock and called urgently to them: *"Ho! Ho! Ho! Taa-taa."* Now that all the sheep could see him, they became calmer.

Soon they all went forward again. "Keep a sharp watch," warned Reuben. The old shepherd's eyes were everywhere. "No evil, for Thou art with me," Azor heard him murmuring, as if thinking out loud. Then Reuben reached for Azor's hand and gave it a little squeeze.

Thy rod and thy staff they comfort me.

It was a slow progress because the path was so rocky. Reuben whistled and called continually. At one place a deep gorge cut the path in two, and the sheep had to jump a few feet to a lower level.

Reuben crossed first. Azor watched while the shepherd laid his staff across the opening and called to the sheep to follow him. The leader sprang over easily, but some needed coaxing, and others, commanding. One timid young sheep missed its footing.

"Oh!" gasped Azor, as he saw it slip to a lower ledge. "How will it ever get out?"

In no time, Reuben had crooked his long staff about the sheep's chest and pulled it up to safety.

"What wonderful things your staff can do," said Azor admiringly.

"Aye, it's my faithful friend," smiled Reuben. "I made it from a sapling oak some forty years ago."

Now the way seemed easier. Surely the dangers were passed. But, looking back, Azor thought he saw a speck in the sky. He tugged at Reuben's sleeve. The shepherd halted, focusing his eyes where Azor pointed.

"You're right, son," he said. "It's an eagle that could carry off a straggling lamb." He paused while the bird sailed nearer. Slowly he drew a stone from his belt and set it in his sling. Then, with a great swing of his arm, he aimed high. The hovering bird swerved and was soon gone. Azor breathed a sigh of relief and felt the warm pressure of Reuben's hand on his shoulder.

Thou preparest a table before me
in the presence of mine enemies.

At last the fine pastures were in sight, and it was sunny again.

"This is beautiful!" Azor shouted, as he ran ahead to pick some wild flowers that he could see growing.

"Wait," called Reuben. There was a snake on a rock. It was a poisonous snake, coiled, ready to strike. With a swift sure blow of his rod, Reuben destroyed it.

"This place is not safe yet. We will go on a little farther," he explained. "There are some plants poisonous to sheep which I must get rid of. You stay with the flock, Azor, while I go ahead."

Feeling sobered and responsible, Azor waited. He picked
up a small rock for defense and kept his eyes alert lest
anything harmful try to approach.

After awhile Reuben returned. They led the sheep
forward.

"What did you do?" asked Azor.

"Grubbed out all those," replied Reuben, pointing to a
pile of rocks on which lay a heap of plants and roots,
wilting in the sun. "Now the pasture is safe for the flock's
last meal—the best grazing of the day."

He looked at the rock in Azor's hand. "That's right," he
said. "You may need it if you see anything harmful. This
is good pasture, but the sheep have many enemies."

The flock grazed. Reuben and Azor kept watch. Back
in the hills a jackal howled hungrily.

Thou anointest my head with oil;
my cup runneth over.

The sun was setting and their shadows lay long before them as Reuben and Azor and the flock walked the last mile back to the sheltering fold for the night. One of the lambs had begun to limp. After examining its sore foot, Reuben picked up the lamb and tucked it inside the front of his tunic. There it rode, with its mother trotting close to Reuben's heels. Occasionally Azor fed it a handful of sweet grass.

"May I carry it awhile?" he asked longingly.

Reuben consented, then showed the boy how to place the lamb on his shoulders. Azor carried it proudly until they reached the familiar stone entrance of the fold, when he set it down by its mother.

"Now to rod them," Reuben said, as he took the leather pouch from Azor and placed his rod across the opening of the fold. Standing there, he called the sheep, counting each one:

"One, two, three, four, five—." As each sheep pressed past him, the old shepherd looked it over carefully, quickly detecting anything wrong. "You have a bad scratch . . . ," he said to one, dropping his rod across its back. "Those poor eyes are weeping," he said to another.

One or two had torn their ears on briars. Reuben made each injured sheep wait outside the fold. When all the rest had safely passed under the rod, he gently attended to the waiting ones.

Azor watched as Reuben poured oil from his ram's horn onto their heads and rubbed it in. With a sharp instrument from his bag he removed a thorn from the lamb's foot, then rubbed cedar tar into wounds and scratches.

"Now, we'll give them a drink," said Reuben. Going to an earthen crock near the wall, he filled a gourd dipper and held it to the first sheep who plunged its nose deep into the cool water till it brimmed over.

"Why, it's right up to the sheep's eyes!" exclaimed Azor.

"That is good, the cup always overflows," replied Reuben. "Now they are ready to join the others," he said, when all the sheep had taken their long deep drink.

*Surely goodness and mercy shall follow me
all the days of my life;
and I will dwell in the house
of the Lord for ever.*

Night was closing down as Reuben and Azor sat on the
ground before the little fire they had made. Reuben said a
simple blessing, then they slowly ate the meal that he had
prepared.

"Tired?" Reuben asked, watching the firelight reflected
in the boy's dark eyes.

"A little," replied Azor, smiling, "but it has been a good
day, hasn't it?" Then he remembered how scared he had
been in the dark valley. "But I wouldn't want to go all
that way alone," he added.

"Nor would the sheep," said Reuben. "But they know they are safe with me, and we are safe with *our* Shepherd, Azor." He paused, listening to the night sounds. His eyes took in the distant view and the first pale stars. "Aye, the house of the Lord is a safe place to be, wherever you find it, son." Quietly, he began to repeat their prayer: "The Lord is my shepherd . . . I shall not want. . . ."

Azor joined in, saying the words slowly with his new friend.

An hour later the fire flickered dimly on the two bundled forms as Reuben, facing the fold, lay across the doorway with Azor close beside him. The sheep were very quiet now. The moon was rising.

"Goodness and mercy," whispered Azor softly to himself, "goodness and mercy—forever."